W9-AAX-574

A Little Bit
of Rob

A Little Bit of Rob

Barbara J. Turner

illustrated by Marni Backer

Albert Whitman & Company

Morton Grove, Illinois

Library of Congress
Cataloging-in-Publication Data

Turner, Barbara J.
A little bit of Rob/written by Barbara J. Turner;
illustrated by Marni Backer.
p.   cm.
Summary: After Rob's death, his parents and
younger sister finally take their boat out crabbing
again in an effort to get their lives back to normal.
ISBN 0-8075-4577-5

[1. Death—Fiction. 2. Brothers and sisters
—Fiction. 3. Crabbing—Fiction.]
I. Backer, Marni, ill. II. Title.
PZ7.T85422Li   1996
[E]—dc20   95-52646
                    CIP
                    AC

Printed in the United States of America.
10 9 8 7 6 5 4 3 2 1

The text typeface is Kennerly.
The illustrations are rendered in oils.
The design is by Scott Piehl.

To my mother, who taught me I could, and to my father, who believed I would. *B.J.T.*

To my mother and father, and my best friends, Noelle and Dave. *M.B.*

WE WENT CRABBING last night—just Mom and Dad and me. It was our first time ever without Rob. Rob was my big brother. He won't be coming with us anymore. He died last month.

Dad steered the *Lena Marie* out into the bay. I watched the city lights shrink in the distance. The tiny lights seemed as far away as Rob.

We followed the sea lanes, weaving between the buoys that marked our way. A big party boat passed by. The people on deck seemed so happy and carefree. They smiled and waved to us as we rocked in their wake. But soon they were gone, and we were alone.

Dad drove the boat a few minutes more. He turned off the engine and dropped the anchor. Above us, a sky full of stars kept watch.

"Go and get the flashlights, Lena," Mom said.

I went below. The cabin reminded me so much of Rob—the bunks where he scared me with ghost stories, the table where we did our homework together, the left-handed reel only Rob could use.

I almost cried.

But I didn't. If I cried, Mom would, too. Maybe even Dad. And we were all trying to be strong. We were all trying to pretend nothing had changed.

I opened the small closet where we kept our supplies. As I reached for the flashlights, I saw Rob's old blue sweatshirt on the floor. I picked it up and held it close. It still smelled like Rob—like outdoors and baseball.

I put the sweatshirt on.

It hung to my knees, but I didn't care. I pushed up the sleeves and grabbed the flashlights.

Mom smiled when she saw me in the
sweatshirt. Her first real smile in weeks.
"I like it," she said.
Dad grinned. "A perfect fit."
I smiled, too.

Mom picked up two nets and passed
one to Dad.

I looked over the side of the boat.
Jellyfish glowed like stars in the dark
water. I reached inside the bait bucket and
threw some sea worms into the ocean.

"One, two, three, shine!" Mom called.

I switched on both flashlights. The
beams skipped over the waves. And there
were the crabs, their snipping claws
snatching at worms.

Mom and Dad swished their nets
through the water. Mom scooped up three
large crabs, Dad two. The others sank
quickly to the safety of the ocean floor.

Dad dumped his crabs into a tub and
passed me the net.

"Your turn, Lena," he said.

I handed Dad the flashlights. He tossed
his handful of sea worms.

"One, two, three, shine!" I called.

I dipped my net into the water and
pulled out some crabs of my own.

"Five, Mom! I caught five! Nobody ever
caught five before! No one except…"

I had almost said it. The name no one
had said these past few weeks.

"No one except Rob?" Mom asked. Her eyes were wet, but there was a smile behind the tears.

I nodded.

"He'd be proud of you, Lena," Dad said, his eyes moist, too.

I grinned and zipped up Rob's sweatshirt. Suddenly, he didn't seem so far away. It was as if he were there on the boat, his arms around me, watching me dip my net, helping me trap the scuttling crabs.

We caught crabs all night long. When our tubs were filled, we headed for shore.

At the dock, we loaded the tubs onto the back of our pick-up and drove to Mr. Hooker's Lobster Barn.

Mr. Hooker weighed the crabs on his big scale. Seventy-two pounds!

"That's a fine night's work, folks," Mr. Hooker said. He gave Dad some money. Dad thanked him, and we left.

On the ride home, I sat between Mom and Dad. The stars were slowly disappearing as the sky turned from black to gray. In the half-light, I noticed how sad my parents looked.

"Dad," I said, "could you pull over, please?"

"Sure, honey," Dad said.

He parked the truck by the curb. "Is something wrong?"

"No," I said. "I just thought we could share for a while. You and Mom need a little bit of Rob, too."

I took off Rob's sweatshirt and spread it over the three of us.

"We'll always have Rob, Lena," Mom said, snuggling closer. "As long as we remember."

"And we'll always remember," Dad said. He squished closer, too.

We stayed that way, nestled together beneath Rob's sweatshirt—crying, remembering Rob, and even laughing once or twice—until the sun rose over the treetops.

It was time to go home.